LiSteN to OUr WorLd

Bill Martin Jr & Michael Sampson

illustrated by Melissa Sweet

A PAULA WISEMAN BOOK
Simon & Schuster Books for Young Readers
New York London Toronto Sydney New Delhi

To my grandson, Reid Sampson
—Michael Sampson

To Lulu and Levi
—Melissa Sweet

In the morning, Mommy gives us
wake-up kisses and says,
"Good morning, little one.
Can you hear the sounds of
our world?"

Listen!
Listen!
Listen!

Near the tall cactus, Gila monsters crawl.

The desert is their world.

High above the mountain peaks, eagles soar.
The wilderness is their world.

Weee-aaa!

Weee-aaa!
Weee-aaa!

In the dense canopy, monkeys swing on vines.
The jungle is their world.

In the green undergrowth, baby pandas chew on sprouts. The bamboo forest is their world.

Grrr. Grrr. Grrr!

In the oozy swamp, crocodiles glide through the algae.
The marshland is their world.

In the grassy savanna, kangaroos hop.
The outback is their world.

On the rolling plain, lions pounce.
The savanna is their world.

On a freezing glacier, black-and-white penguins waddle.
The South Pole is their world.

In the refreshing oasis, elephants find cool water.
The grassland is their world.

In the blue sea, whales swim through the waves.
The ocean is their world.

At night, Mommy gives us good-night kisses and says,
"Sweet dreams, my little ones. All is well in our world."

Hush...
hush...
hush...

FACTS ABOUT THE ANIMALS IN THIS BOOK

GILA MONSTER

Habitat: the desert

Gila monsters are lizards that live in the Southwestern United States and the Mexican state of Sonora. They are poisonous but slow, and rarely bite humans. The Gila monster in this book lives in the Sonoran Desert in Mexico, in North America.

PARROT

Habitat: tropical rain forests

Parrots live in the tropical rain forest and like to fly around giant kapok trees. The colorful parrot in this book lives in Brazil, in South America.

EAGLE

Habitat: mountains and lake regions

Eagles live in many places in the world and love to soar above mountains and lakes. The bald eagle in this book lives in Alaska, in the United States, in North America.

MONKEY

Habitat: tropical rain forests

Monkeys live in many places in the world and love to swing from vine to vine. The monkeys in this book live in Costa Rica, in Central America.

GIANT PANDA

Habitat: bamboo forests

Pandas live in bamboo forests and love to chew bamboo sprouts. The giant panda in this book lives in China, in Asia.

CROCODILE

Habitat: marshlands

Crocodiles live in tropical climates and love to lie still and pretend to be logs. The crocodiles in this book live in the Dominican Republic, in the Caribbean Sea.

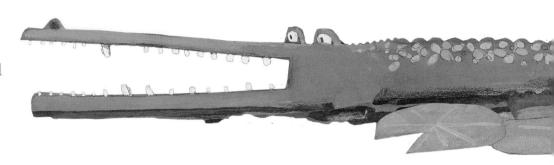

KANGAROO

Habitat: the outback

Kangaroos live in Australia on high plains called the outback. Female kangaroos carry their babies in a pouch on their stomachs. The red kangaroos in this book live near the rangelands of western New South Wales, in Australia.

LION

Habitat: the plains

Lions live in Africa. They travel in families called prides. The lions in this book live near Kenya, in Africa.

PENGUIN

Habitat: Southern Hemisphere

Penguins live on every continent in the Southern Hemisphere. The male emperor penguin holds the egg in his feet and covers it with his warm feathers while the female hunts for food. The penguins in this book live in Antarctica, near the South Pole.

ELEPHANT

Habitat: grasslands

Elephants live in Africa and Asia. They have a very long nose, called a trunk, which they can use like a hose to wash their young. The animals in this book live near Namibia, in Africa.

WHALE

Habitat: the ocean

Whales live in every ocean of the world. They are mammals and breathe air, and like to blow the water out of their air tubes. The whales in this book live in the Atlantic Ocean, near Maine, in North America.

CHILD

Children live all over the world. They love to play and laugh. The children in this book may live near you!

SIMON & SCHUSTER BOOKS FOR YOUNG READERS

An imprint of Simon & Schuster Children's Publishing Division

1230 Avenue of the Americas, New York, New York 10020

Text copyright © 2016 by Michael Sampson

Illustrations copyright © 2016 by Melissa Sweet

SIMON & SCHUSTER BOOKS FOR YOUNG READERS is a trademark of Simon & Schuster, Inc.

For information about special discounts for bulk purchases, please contact Simon & Schuster Special Sales at 1-866-506-1949 or business@simonandschuster.com.

The Simon & Schuster Speakers Bureau can bring authors to your live event. For more information or to book an event, contact the Simon & Schuster Speakers Bureau at 1-866-248-3049 or visit our website at www.simonspeakers.com.

Book design by Krista Vossen

The text for this book is set in Filosofia.

The illustrations for this book are rendered in watercolor, handmade papers, and mixed media.

Manufactured in China

0816 SCP

4 6 8 10 9 7 5 3

Library of Congress Cataloging-in-Publication Data

Martin, Bill, 1916–2004, author.

Listen to our world / Bill Martin, Jr, Michael Sampson ; illustrated by Melissa Sweet. — First edition.

pages cm

"A Paula Wiseman Book."

Summary: Youngsters awaken in the morning with the belief that they are the greatest little ones in the world, whether they are children in their mothers' arms, eagles soaring above mountains, whales swimming in the ocean, or other animals in their domains.

ISBN 978-1-4424-5472-9 (hardcover) — ISBN 978-1-4424-5473-6 (eBook)

[1. Animals—Habitations—Fiction.] I. Sampson, Michael R., author. II. Sweet, Melissa, 1956– illustrator. III. Title.

PZ7.M356773Lf 2016

[E]—dc23

2015004925